CREATURE CARNIVAL

BY MARILYN SINGER

ILLUSTRATIONS BY GRIS GRIMLY

HYPERION BOOKS FOR CHILDREN
NEW YORK

To Donna Bray, who appreciates all kinds of creatures
—M.S.

Hats off to Tod Browning and the cast of *Freaks*, who taught
me about acceptance . . . "One of us! One of us!"
—G.G.

Acknowledgments
Thanks to Steve Aronson, Dave Lubar, Asher Williams, and the gang at Hyperion.
—M.S.

First Edition
3 5 7 9 10 8 6 4 2
This book is set in Alcoholica Regular and Mister Frisky.
Handlettering by Gris Grimly
Reinforced binding

ISBN 0-7868-1877-8
Library of Congress Cataloging-in-Publication Data on file.
Visit www.hyperionchildrensbooks.com

Dresses funny,
Basket's runny:
Overworked Easter Bunny.

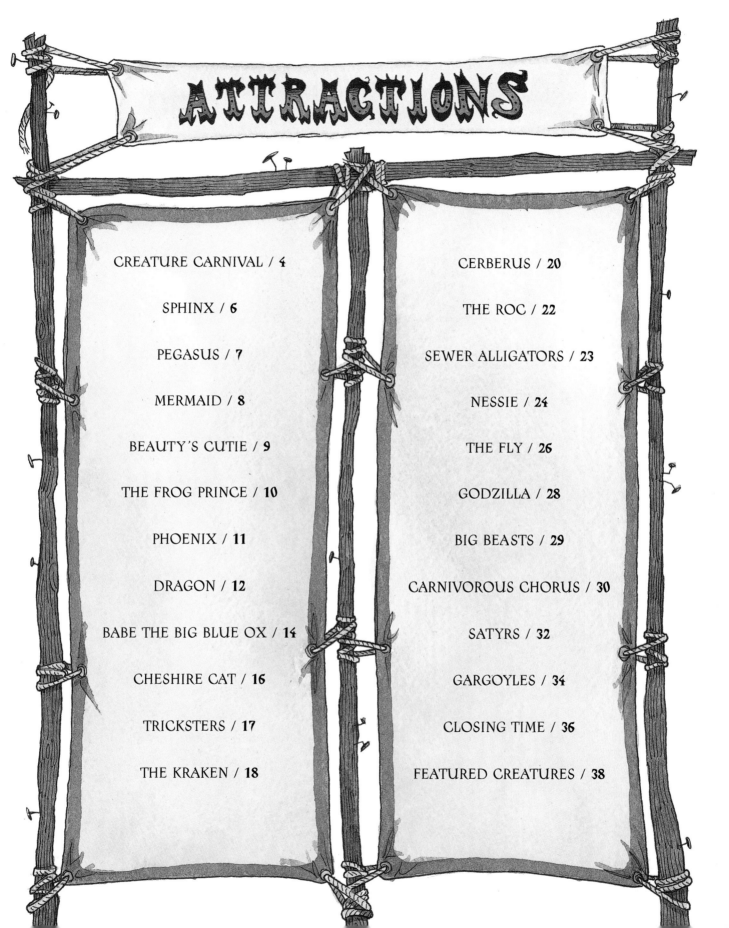

ATTRACTIONS

CREATURE CARNIVAL

Come along, children of all ages.
See fabled beasts not found in cages.
Spend your parents' hard-earned wages.
    It's Creature Carnival time.

Here be dragons, aye, forsooth!
And a sphinx who's quite uncouth.
You'll like the Frog Prince kissing booth.
    It's Creature Carnival time.

Our flying horse suggests you duck.
Brer Rabbit says, "Hey, try your luck."
Then watch Godzilla stomp a truck.
    It's Creature Carnival time.

4

Listen—that's the werewolf's band
over by the I Scream stand.
Ticket, please. I'll stamp your hand.
You'll have thrills and chills and slime,
See a mermaid in her prime.
At Creature Carn—
(What's that roaring in the barn?)
At Creature Carnival time!

SPHINX

If she's lyin'
     like a lion
but she's acting
     like a minx,
She's a sphinx.
If she wearies
     with her queries
and she stares
     but never blinks,
She's a sphinx.
She's a dweller of the desert
     where it's hotter than a griddle.
And I'll bet you she'll upset you
     if you cannot guess her riddle.
So please avoid
     or be destroyed
by such an antiquated jinx.
     (She really stinks!)
She's a sphinx!

PEGASUS

Has hooves, has mane,
Has tail, can neigh.
Has wings, can fly,
Might nest in hay.
Not a horse, not a bird,
Wouldn't drop an egg on us.
Very sleek, very Greek,
In a word:

it's Pegasus.

MERMAID

I want to be Miss Ocean.
I want to see me crowned,
     blow kisses at the judges.
(There're three of them I've drowned.)

I want to be Miss Ocean.
My mom and dad would flip.
     I'll win the talent contest
And sink another ship.

I've been Miss Cove, Miss Coral Reef,
Miss Bay, Miss Briny Breeze.
     But I can't rest until I'm best—
The Queen of Seven Seas.

I want to be Miss Ocean.
I've got the nicest fins.
     Besides, I'll cut her hair off
If another mermaid wins.

8

BEAUTY'S CUTIE

It matters not that he's rather furry.
It matters not that he's got big claws.
So what if when he drinks, he dribbles?
So what if when he eats, he gnaws?
I do not care that his teeth are pointy
Or that his growl makes Father wince.
So many princes turn out beastly.
How pleasant that my Beast's
     a prince.

THROW A HORSESHOE
WIN A PRIZE!!

THE FROG PRINCE

Forget a duck or armadillo—
    let a froggie share your pillow.
I hardly take up any space.
I'll chase mosquitoes from your face.
I'm quite a charming shade of green.
I always keep my toenails clean.
I'll sing you songs and tell you tales
    of big bad wolves and hungry whales.
If I should change, you'd surely miss me.
So, princess dear, don't ever

              kiss me!

Kisses 50¢

10

PHOENIX

No duet was ever sweeter
  than Phoenix and her fire-eater.
From the pyre where she wallows,
  he gathers golden flames and swallows.
When she rises, how she chirps
  at the smoke rings that he burps.

DRAGON

Flappiness,
Sappiness:
Bluebird of Happiness.

You can't domesticate a dragon.
He'll never pull a plow or wagon.
He has no wool, he can't make silk.
His looks alone would curdle milk.
He will not let you take a ride.
Try saddling him and you'll get fried.
He can't herd sheep or hunt a mouse.
He's liable to burn down your house.
He's fond of gold, he's pleased by pearls—
    and sometimes he eats boys and girls.
But we would not be so beguiled
    if dragons weren't oh-so-wild.

BABE THE BIG BLUE OX

There's a fracas, there's a ruckus,
    and it's causing lots of shocks—
They're taking the blue ribbon back
    from Babe the Big Blue Ox.
She pulled and pulled a mighty load.
    She did it fair and square.
But, you see, it was a team event—
    and she's just half a pair.

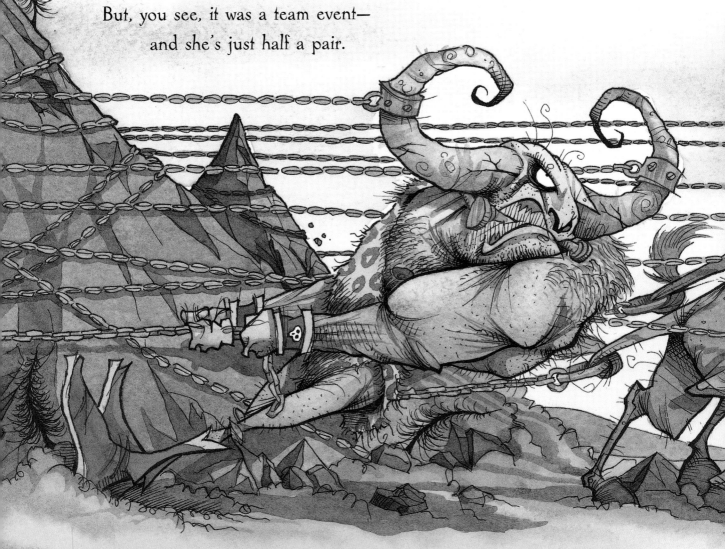

14

The top judge shook his head and sighed,
"Those are the rules, I fear."
Paul Bunyan stroked his beard and smiled.
"I've got me an idea."
He rounded up two Cretan bulls
and one horned Minotaur.
Oh, how they aced it, they first-placed it—
that bovine team of four!

CHESHIRE CAT

I'm not known for
        my fur
or my purr,
        how I growl,
how I prowl,
        for catching mice,
or being nice.
It's the style
        of my smile
you'll remember for years:
        wide and gloating,
calmly floating.
It's the best of me
    while the rest of me
        oh-so-slowly
            disappears. . . .

TRICKSTERS

Take my advice and don't let down your guard
    with Old Man Coyote or Monsieur Reynard.
Likewise, I'd say that it's not a good habit
    to trust anyone by the name Brer Rabbit.
A leopard I met says it's equally chancy
    to listen to tales by that spider Anansi.
They'll amuse you, confuse you, and here's the big news:
    With tricksters, my friend, you are certain to lose
        your money, your honey,
            and even your shoes.

THE KRAKEN

Don't ever knock the Kraken.
Don't make fun of his size.
Don't titter at his fishy breath—
　　　it really isn't wise.

Don't ever mock the Kraken.
Don't joke about his arms.
Don't tell him he's a *sucker*
　　　who's *stuck* on all your charms.

Don't try to block the Kraken.
He makes an awful catch.
Believe me, kid,
That giant squid
　　　wins every wrestling match!

CERBERUS

Hurry, hurry, kids, gents, ladies!
Step inside the gates of Hades!
There'll be thrills, there'll be chills
in this land of the dead,
And you'll get to pet Cerberus
on the head
head
and head.

We can guarantee kicks
when he shows off his tricks—
Fetching three balls at once
from the deep River Styx.
Such an excellent pooch,
but with one fault, alas—
You must toss him a treat
if you're eager to pass.
For no matter how often
he tries and he tries,
He's no good with hellos—
and he's worse with good-byes.

20

When meeting this bird face-to-face,
You must give yourself plenty of space.
     You'll be quite out of luck
     If by chance you get stuck
'Tween a roc and a very hard place.

22

SEWER ALLIGATORS

If "toilet" and "flush"
    often cause you to blush,
If cold-blooded pets
    make you break out in sweats,
    or reduce you to tears,
Better cover your ears.
I'm not talking hippos,
I'm not talking rhinos,
I'm speaking of gators—
    a bunch of albinos!
Down in the sewers
    there isn't much light,
So all of these critters
    were bound to turn white.
Such a sad fate,
    for they once were deep green.
Come see for yourself
    why it's wrong to be mean
And exile a reptile
    down someone's latrine.

23

NESSIE

Thousands of miles
>   from the fair Loch Ness banks,
Swimming in one
>   of the world's largest tanks,
(You can feed her some fishes,
>   but don't expect thanks)
This way to our greatest attraction!
Is she chartreuse
>   or is she vermilion?
Is she amphibious?
>   Is she reptilian?
Is she just one—
>   or just one in a million?
She stirs up a major reaction!
Holding her breath?
>   She can do it with ease.
(Though there is some concern
>   if she happens to sneeze.)
Stay away from the edge
>   and no flash pictures, please.
You might glimpse the tiniest fraction.
>   (No refunds for dissatisfaction.)
This way to see Nessie in action!

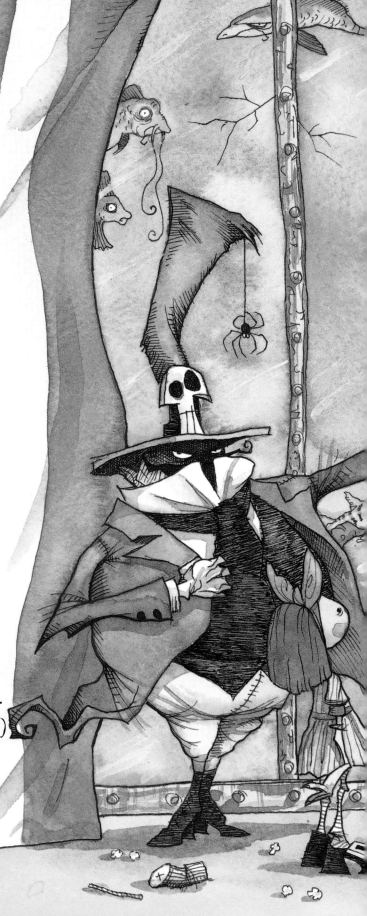

Nocturnal fowl,
Stuck on a vowel:
Wise old owl.

25

THE FLY

DR. LANGELAAN

I was once a scientist.
My keen machine performed a twist.
I'm crossed off every Christmas list.
'Cause I'm The Fly.
I was a guy—
        now I'm The Fly.

Dining out was once a breeze.
No one thought I was a sleaze.
Today I've joined a troop of fleas.
'Cause I'm The Fly.
I was a guy—
        now I'm The Fly.

It made me glad
        to be called mad,
        to live among outsiders.
But things have changed—
        I'm rearranged,
        and oh-so-scared of spiders.

26

Bend down closer. Can you spot me?
Watch that web—it nearly got me.
And for heaven's sake, don't swat me!
Don't wanna die,
	though I'm The Fly.
To clarify:
	Can't wear a tie,
	Can't bake a pie,
	I'm quite sci-fi.
I was a guy—
	now I'm The Fly.

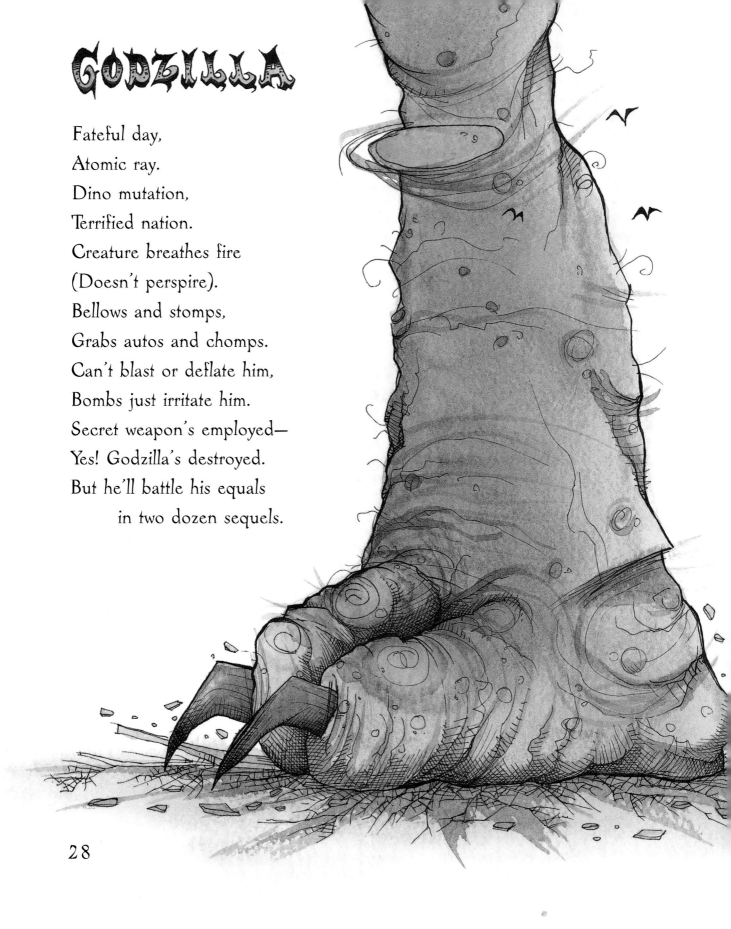

GODZILLA

Fateful day,
Atomic ray.
Dino mutation,
Terrified nation.
Creature breathes fire
(Doesn't perspire).
Bellows and stomps,
Grabs autos and chomps.
Can't blast or deflate him,
Bombs just irritate him.
Secret weapon's employed—
Yes! Godzilla's destroyed.
But he'll battle his equals
    in two dozen sequels.

BIG BEASTS

Behemoth and Leviathan are having quite a fight.
Each claims to be the biggest—
    but which of them is right?
One's larger than the largest barge,
One's greater than a freighter.
But who has got a scale to gauge
    the greatest heavyweighter?

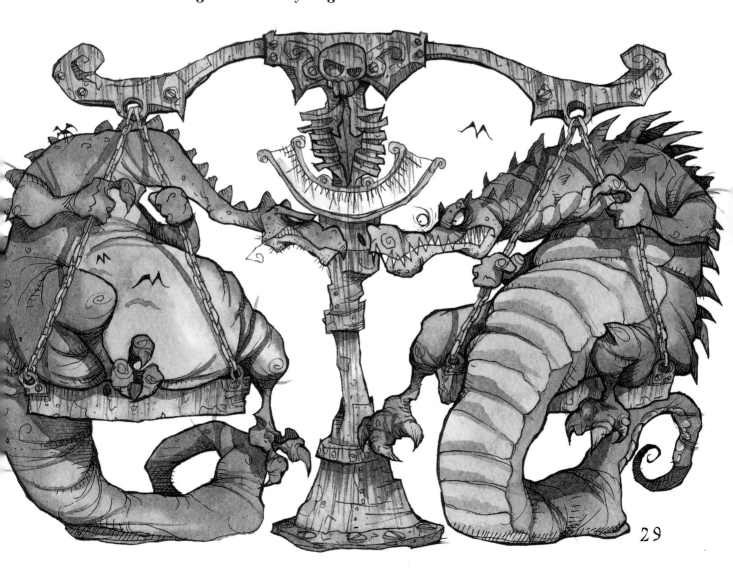

CARNIVOROUS CHORUS

No words found in any thesaurus
    describe our carnivorous chorus.
The harpies are shrieking
    a murderous tune.
The werewolf is clearing
    his throat at the moon.
The manticore trills
    like a trumpet and flute.
(It's hard to believe he's a man-eating brute.)
The sirens sound lovely,
    their song so alluring.
Fans drown in their sound
    wherever they're touring.
We've got special box seats
    in a really strong cage.
(I wouldn't advise sitting close to the stage.)
Be brave and come rave
    with your favorite beast.
But exit at once
    when it threatens to feast.

SATYRS

Bow to your partner,
    don't be aloof.
Bow to your corner,
    watch that hoof.
Do-si-do—
    let's raise the roof!
Doing the satyr square dance.

Promenade all,
    right up the middle.
Pan's on the pipes
    and cat's on the fiddle.

Everyone's cooking
    like a red-hot griddle.
Doing the satyr square dance.

Swing your partner
    till she floats.
Allemande left,
    then eat your oats.
Oh, what a graceful group
    of goats!
Doing the satyr,
Doing the satyr,
Doing the satyr
    square dance!

GARGOYLES

Do you want to see a griffon
    unstiffen?
Do you want to spy a wyvern
    revive?
Bears and monkeys made of stone—
Watch them change to flesh and bone,
In the hour when the gargoyles come
    alive.

Would you care to have a statue
    try and catch you?
Would you like to watch a rainspout
    mobilize?
From great palaces and churches,
Swans and eagles leave their perches,
In the hour when the gargoyles
    seize the skies.

Two free tickets to the show
        if you buy the video—
At just nineteen ninety-five it's quite a steal.
Full of petrifying news,
        lots of monstrous interviews,
Sixty minutes—
Feel the power,
        of that dark, fantastic hour
When the gargoyles all turn
        absolutely real.

CLOSING TIME

The lovely mermaid has stopped posing.
The sweaty satyrs need a hosing.
The gates of Hades—hear them closing?
    Good-bye, Creature Carnival time!

    The Big Blue Ox has finished hauling.
    The Minotaur has started sprawling.
    Godzilla's done his daily mauling.
        Farewell, Creature Carnival time!

No creature can be creepy
    when it's feeling rather sleepy.
So to act its beastly best,
    it must get a proper rest.

    The horrid harpies are widely yawning.
    The gargoyles are awake and spawning.
    A brand-new day will soon be dawning,
            with shouts and routs sublime
            and a healthy dash of grime.

36

But for now, ta-ta, *adieu*,
   buenas noches, ciao to you.
Bing-bong, the closing bell
   begins to chime.
So long, Creature Carnival time!

37

FEATURED CREATURES

ANANSI: Sometimes foolish, sometimes wise, this African spider tricks friends and neighbors out of drums, stories, and other goodies. He often gets away with it—but not always. He's been known to help people, teaching them to plow fields and plant grain.

BABE THE BIG BLUE OX: Pet of Paul Bunyan, the greatest lumberjack who ever lived, Babe is the world's biggest, strongest ox. When the pair traveled up and down Minnesota, Babe's footprints created 10,000 lakes.

BEAUTY'S BEAST: Once a handsome prince until an evil spell turned him beastly, the Beast is lonely and sad until Beauty shows up at his palace. He treats her so well that she falls in love with him and breaks the spell. And yes, they do live happily ever after.

BEHEMOTH: A gigantic beast mentioned in the Bible. Its bones are as strong as iron and it can drink up a whole river. It lives on land and may resemble a hippopotamus. It detests the **Leviathan**.

BLUEBIRD OF HAPPINESS: This bringer of good cheer was introduced by Maurice Maeterlinck in *The Bluebird*. In this play, two kids search for the bird only to find it—and happiness—in their own backyard.

BRER RABBIT: A trickster from West Africa by way of the American South, Brer Rabbit is no cuddly bunny. He'll fool foxes, bears, and you, if he can, taking your food, your money, and your dignity.

CERBERUS: Most dogs have one head. This one has three. He guards the gates of Hades, entrance to the Greek underworld. He lets new spirits enter this land of the dead, but he will not let them out.

CHESHIRE CAT: Direct from Wonderland, Alice's loony feline friend is famous for fading from sight, leaving behind a huge grin.

COYOTE: A cocky canine of Western and Southwestern Native American tales, Coyote will fool—or be fooled. Like Anansi, he's sometimes kind to humans, creating animals for them to hunt and protecting them from evil spirits.

CRETAN BULL: When Poseidon, the Greek god of the sea, asked King Minos of Crete to sacrifice this bull, the king refused. The angry god made the bull run wild all over the island. He also caused Minos's wife, Pasiphae, to fall in love with it. She soon gave birth to their half-bull, half-human son, the **Minotaur**.

DRAGON: Perhaps the most famous of all fabulous creatures, this scaly flying reptile is found everywhere. In Asia, dragons bring rain and good fortune. In Europe, they hoard treasure, breathe fire, burn towns, and eat people. Knights went on quests to hunt dragons. Some didn't come back.

38

EASTER BUNNY: Centuries ago, German children believed in a magical hare that left them a nest of colored eggs at Eastertime. When the Germans came to America in the 1700s, they brought the Easter bunny with them.

THE FLY: Featured in several movies, this poor fellow was once a scientist until he got scrambled in a transporter. Now he's half man, half fly. No swatters, please!

FROG PRINCE: Another beast under another spell, this amphibian rescued a princess's ball from a well. As his reward, he asked her to let him sleep on her pillow and then give him a kiss. When she gave in, *poof!*—another handsome prince!

GARGOYLES: Stone guardians of palaces and churches, these bizarre creatures come to life only at night. Among the types of gargoyles are **griffons** (part eagle, part lion, sometimes part snake) and **wyverns** (two-legged dragons). Gargoyles also do a great job of draining rainwater from buildings.

GODZILLA: A big star of the screen, Godzilla has stomped and chomped his way through two dozen movies. In Japan, where he was born, this mutated dinosaur goes by the name Gojira.

HARPIES: Dirty and very smelly, harpies have hideous faces of women and bodies of vultures. They snatch food and souls with their sharp claws, then fly away, shrieking.

KRAKEN: This giant many-armed squid found in Scandinavian waters pretends to be an island. When a ship approaches, the Kraken grabs and drags it to the bottom of the sea. Perhaps it mistakes a ship for one of its favorite finger foods—a whale.

LEVIATHAN: Another enormous beast of the Bible. This one lives in the ocean and may look like a whale. It can't stand the **Behemoth**.

LOCH NESS MONSTER: Nicknamed "Nessie," this shy creature, found in a Scottish lake, is occasionally seen, but rarely photographed. Is she a sea serpent? A plesiosaur? A giant amphibian? A huge fish? Fame and fortune to whoever solves the mystery!

MANTICORE: A man-eating beast with a man's head, lion's body, and scorpion's stinger. The Manticore has a lovely voice, which sounds like a combination of pipes and trumpet.

MERMAID: A woman from the waist up, fish from the waist down, a mermaid spends a lot of time gazing into a mirror and combing her long hair. Some mermaids rescue men; others lure men to their death. All of them are beautiful—and most of them know it!

MINOTAUR: Son of Queen Pasiphae and the Cretan Bull, this monster was shut up in the Labyrinth, a huge maze beneath the palace, by King Minos. Every year, the Minotaur ate several prisoners until the Greek hero Theseus killed it, giving rise to the idea that Greek mythology is full of bull.

OWL: Supposedly smart, but isn't. It got that reputation because it sits still during the day and appears to be thinking deep thoughts.

PEGASUS: This beautiful flying horse sprang from the blood of the monstrous snake-haired Medusa. The Greek hero Bellerophon managed to capture Pegasus. He rode the horse when he went to kill another monster—the lion-goat-snake Chimera.

PHOENIX: A spectacular bird with a lovely voice, the Phoenix can live hundreds or even thousands of years. Then it sets fire to its nest and burns up, only to be reborn as a magnificent new bird.

REYNARD: This sly fox of France is the main character of songs and stories dating back to the Middle Ages. He's especially talented at getting other creatures to do his work.

ROC: This enormous bird can carry an elephant in its claws. Sinbad the Sailor from *The Arabian Nights* was stranded in a roc's nest on top of a mountain. Using his turban, he tied himself to the roc's leg. Then he dropped off when the bird passed over another island, making himself a candidate for the Roc and Roll Hall of Fame.

SATYRS: Hairy, wild creatures, half man, half goat. They love to drink and dance. Pan, the best-known satyr, plays music on his seven-reed pipes. When he and his friends get too crazy, they cause a *panic*.

SEWER ALLIGATORS: Unloved, unwanted pets flushed down the toilet, these urban legends survive and thrive in the city sewers on a diet of rats and other delicacies. But it would be cruel to return them to their swamps. Pure white from lack of light, the poor things would get sunburned.

SIRENS: Half bird, half woman, these creatures live on an island near Italy. Their songs are so enchanting, they make sailors lose control and crash their ships into the rocks. The Greek hero Odysseus and his crew escaped the sirens. Under his command, the sailors put beeswax in their ears and tied the captain to a mast so he wouldn't go mad and jump ship.

SPHINX: Part lion, part woman, all bad temper. In ancient Greece, she asked travelers to answer a riddle: "What walks on four legs in the morning, two legs at midday, and three legs at night?" [See below for answer.*] Those who guessed wrong were killed. When Oedipus finally answered correctly, she jumped off a cliff. In Egypt, a stone sphinx guards the pyramids.

WEREWOLF: This howler changes from human to wolf during a full moon. Unlike real wolves, werewolves will hunt humans.

* **Sphinx's Riddle:** The answer is **human being** (a baby on four legs, a grown-up on two, an old person with a cane on three).